THE TIGER AND THE WOODPECKER

ONE DAY, AS A TIGER WAS DEVOURING THE GAME HE HAD KILLED, A BONE STUCK IN HIS JAW. A WOODPECKER, WHO LIVED IN THE BRANCHES ABOVE, WATCHED HIM.

TRY AS IT MIGHT, HE COULD NOT GET THE BONE UNSTUCK.

I WILL NOT BE ABLE TO EAT ANYTHING UNLESS I GET THIS BONE OUT.

DAYS PASSED. HE BECAME WEAKER AND WEAKER.

IF SOMEONE DOES NOT COME TO HELP ME, I WILL SOON DIE OF STARVATION.

THE WOODPECKER WAS PUZZLED.

WHAT'S THE MATTER WITH YOU? WHY DO YOU LIE THERE WITH YOUR MOUTH OPEN?

THE TIGER BECKONED TO THE WOODPECKER TO COME NEAR...

...AND POINTED TO THE BONE IN HIS MOUTH.

OH! OH! IT'S A BONE. I SHALL REMOVE IT...IF YOU WILL GIVE ME MY FILL OF THE FLESH OF THE ANIMALS YOU KILL.

THE TIGER NODDED HIS HEAD.

THE WOODPECKER FLEW INTO THE TIGER'S MOUTH...

...PULLED OUT THE BONE...

...CAME OUT OF THE TIGER'S MOUTH AT FULL SPEED...

...FLEW UP TO THE TREE...

...AND PERCHING THERE, DROPPED THE BONE.

A FEW HOURS LATER, THE TIGER KILLED AN ANIMAL AND BEGAN DEVOURING IT.

THE TIGER LOOKED AT THE WOODPECKER AND PRETENDED HE HAD NEVER SEEN HIM BEFORE.

WHO ARE YOU? WHY SHOULD I OFFER YOU ANY PART OF THIS?

THE WOODPECKER WAS SHOCKED.

WHAT!

DON'T YOU REMEMBER ME? I PULLED OUT THE BONE FROM YOUR MOUTH. HOW COULD YOU FORGET ME SO SOON?

THE TIGER LAUGHED.

YOU KNOW I AM A WILD ANIMAL. I COULD EASILY HAVE EATEN YOU WHEN YOU ENTERED MY MOUTH. I DIDN'T. BE GRATEFUL FOR THAT AND BEGONE!

THE END

5

THE CLEVER TURTLE

LONG AGO, THERE LIVED A FEW TURTLES ON A SEA COAST. EVERY DAY AN EAGLE USED TO CATCH ONE OF THEM FOR FOOD.

THIS WORRIED AN AGED TURTLE.

AT THIS RATE, NOT ONE OF US WILL BE LEFT ALIVE.

WE MUST DO SOMETHING TO SAVE OURSELVES.

HE WITHDREW INTO HIS SHELL AND BEGAN TO THINK HARD.

WHY, THAT'S IT! WHY DIDN'T I THINK OF IT BEFORE!

6

HE CALLED A MEETING OF THE SURVIVING TURTLES.

IF YOU DO AS I SAY, WE CAN GET RID OF THE EAGLE FOR GOOD.

WE'LL DO ANYTHING YOU SAY TO SAVE OUR LIVES.

ALL RIGHT. THEN HIDE YOURSELVES IN THE WATER WHEN YOU SEE THE EAGLE TOMORROW.

THE NEXT DAY, WHEN THE EAGLE SWOOPED DOWN AS USUAL—

QUICK! INTO THE WATER.

WHEN THE EAGLE CAME NEARER—

O EAGLE, ALL MY RELATIVES HAVE BEEN DEVOURED BY YOU. I AM THE ONLY ONE LEFT NOW.

POST YOURSELVES IN THE WATER IN A STRAIGHT LINE AT EQUAL DISTANCES. AS THE EAGLE FLIES OVER YOU, RAISE YOUR HEAD AND SHOW YOURSELVES.

THE TURTLES ACCORDINGLY TOOK THEIR POSITIONS IN THE WATER.

A WEEK LATER, THE RACE BETWEEN THE EAGLE AND THE TURTLE BEGAN.

ARE YOU READY?

LET'S GO.

THE EAGLE FLEW WITH GREAT SPEED BUT...

...THE TURTLE SEEMED TO BE ALWAYS AHEAD OF HIM BY MILES.

I CANNOT KEEP IT UP ANY LONGER. BUT THE TURTLE SEEMS FRESH AS EVER.

NO. I CANNOT. LET ME FLY AWAY TO A TREE ON SHORE BEFORE I FALL DOWN EXHAUSTED.

THE NEXT DAY, HE CAME TO SEE THE OLD TURTLE.

YOU WIN. I WILL NEVER EAT ANOTHER TURTLE IN MY LIFE.

THE END

THE HARE, THE PARTRIDGE AND THE TIGER

ON THE BANKS OF THE NARMADA WAS A FOREST. THE ANIMALS WHO LIVED THERE WERE ALWAYS QUARRELLING.

WE QUARREL BECAUSE WE HAVE NO KING TO SETTLE OUR DISPUTES.

YES. WE SHOULD HAVE A KING.

BUT WHO WILL BE THE KING?

PANDEMONIUM BROKE OUT.

I WILL BE THE KING.

NOT YOU. I WILL BE THE KING.

IT SHOULD BE ME.

11

AN OLD AND INFIRM TIGER, WHO HAD RECENTLY MIGRATED TO THAT FOREST WAS ROUSED FROM HIS SLUMBER.

WHERE IS THIS NOISE FROM? LET ME SEE.

WHEN THE ANIMALS SAW THE OLD TIGER APPROACHING—

WHY DON'T WE MAKE HIM OUR KING?

A GOOD IDEA.

SO WHEN THE OLD TIGER CAME TO THEM—

WE NEED A KING. WILL YOU BE OUR KING AND RULE OVER US?

I CAN'T BELIEVE MY GOOD LUCK! MY DAYS OF STARVATION ARE OVER.

I DO NOT MIND BEING KING. BUT I DISLIKE VIOLENCE. SO I WILL KILL ONLY IF IT IS ABSOLUTELY NECESSARY, AFTER MAKING A CAREFUL STUDY OF EACH CASE.

THE ANIMALS WERE DELIGHTED.

O KING, WE TOO DISLIKE AND FEAR VIOLENCE. BUT A JUST KING HAS TO KILL THE GUILTY ONES.

AND MOST OF THE TIME I WILL FIND IT NECESSARY.

THE VERY NEXT DAY, A HARE AND A PARTRIDGE HAD A BITTER QUARREL.

THIS HOLE IS MINE.

NO, IT IS MINE! I FOUND IT FIRST.

YOU FOUND IT ALL RIGHT. BUT IT WAS MY FATHER WHO MADE IT.

BUT YOUR FATHER ABANDONED IT. I MOVED IN. SO IT'S MINE.

THE HARE WAS QUIET FOR A MOMENT. THEN AN IDEA STRUCK HIM.

LET'S GO TO OUR KING! LET HIM DECIDE TO WHOM IT BELONGS.

FAIR ENOUGH. WE'LL GO TO HIM.

13

SO THEY WENT TO THE OLD TIGER.

O KING, WE SEEK JUSTICE.

WHY? WHAT'S THE MATTER?

THE TWO CREATURES BEGAN EXPLAINING THE SITUATION AT THE SAME TIME.

JUST A MINUTE. I AM OLD AND CAN'T HEAR PROPERLY. COME CLOSER AND EXPLAIN THE CASE TO ME.

AS SOON AS THE UNSUSPECTING ANIMALS CAME CLOSE TO THE TIGER, HE SPRANG ON THEM...

...AND DEVOURED THEM.

IF ONLY WE HAD SETTLED OUR OWN DISPUTES INSTEAD OF INVITING A STRANGER TO SETTLE THEM FOR US.

THE END

THE SERPENT AND THE RAT

A SNAKE-CHARMER ONCE CAUGHT A SERPENT AND PUT IT INTO A CANE BASKET.

THEN HE CAUGHT A RAT AND PUT IT INTO THE BASKET, TOO.

THERE! THAT SHOULD MAKE A FINE MEAL FOR MY SERPENT.

BUT WHEN THE SERPENT CAME NEAR THE RAT TO EAT IT—

PLEASE SPARE MY LIFE! I CAN FREE YOU.

THE SERPENT WAS AMUSED.

HOW CAN YOU SUCCEED WHERE I HAVE FAILED. BESIDES, I'M TERRIBLY HUNGRY.

THEN WHAT'S THE USE OF EATING ME? I CAN HARDLY SATISFY YOUR HUNGER. IF YOU SPARE MY LIFE, I CAN LEAD YOU OUT TO GET ALL THE FOOD YOU NEED.

BETTER FOOD PERHAPS, FROGS, LIZARDS, PLUMPER RATS THAN ME...

HE IS RIGHT. BESIDES, I CAN EAT HIM AS WELL, LATER.

ALL RIGHT. I WILL NOT EAT YOU. TELL ME HOW YOU CAN GET ME OUT.

I SHALL CHANT A MANTRA SITTING ON YOUR HEAD.

AS SOON AS IT IS OVER I SHALL CALL YOU. TILL THEN YOU SHOULD CLOSE YOUR EYES AND STAY STILL.

I'LL DO AS YOU SAY. BUT PLEASE WAIT FOR ME OUTSIDE.

THE SERPENT THEN CLOSED HIS EYES. THE RAT JUMPED ONTO HIS HEAD...

...GNAWED A HOLE IN THE BOX...

...AND ESCAPED THROUGH IT.

A LITTLE LATER THE SERPENT OPENED HIS EYES AND...

...HE TOO SLID OUT OF THE HOLE IN THE BOX.

AH! IT'S GOOD TO BE FREE. BUT I'M STILL HUNGRY. WHERE IS THE RAT?

IN VAIN DID HE LOOK AROUND FOR THE RAT.

THE WRETCH HAS RUN AWAY! BUT I'LL FIND HIM SOON.

A FEW DAYS LATER, THE SNAKE FOUND THE HOLE IN WHICH THE RAT WAS LIVING.

AH! THERE HE IS, THE CHEAT. THIS TIME HE WON'T ESCAPE.

O RAT, WHY DID YOU RUN AWAY BEFORE I COULD THANK YOU? COME OUT NOW. AREN'T WE FRIENDS?

WE ARE NOT. YOU ARE MY ENEMY AND WILL EAT ME UP. I PRETENDED TO BE YOUR FRIEND ONLY TO SAVE MY LIFE.

FRIENDSHIP IS ONLY BETWEEN EQUALS. I AM NOT YOUR EQUAL, SO WE CAN NEVER BE FRIENDS.

HE IS TOO WISE FOR ME. I'D BETTER GO AND LOOK FOR SOMETHING TO EAT ELSEWHERE.

THE END

THE FOOLISH BRAHMAN

A LEARNED BRAHMAN NAMED GARGYA ONCE WENT FROM HIS VILLAGE TO A FOREST, TO WORSHIP GODDESS DURGA.

PLEASED WITH HIS DEVOTION, THE GODDESS APPEARED BEFORE HIM.

O PIOUS BRAHMAN, YOU DESERVE A BOON. ASK FOR ONE.

O GODDESS, PLEASE GRANT ME THE SANJEEVANI. *

THE GODDESS HELD OUT SOME GREEN LEAVES.

WHENEVER YOU WANT TO BRING THE DEAD BACK TO LIFE, ALL YOU NEED DO IS SPRINKLE THE SAP OF THESE LEAVES ON THE CORPSE.

THE BODY THUS RAISED WILL BE STRONGER AND MORE VIGOROUS THAN BEFORE.

✱ A HERB WHICH IS CREDITED WITH THE POWER TO REVIVE THE DEAD.

BESIDES, THESE LEAVES WILL NEITHER WITHER NOR CHANGE.

'AND THE GODDESS DISAPPEARED.

GARGYA WAS VERY HAPPY AS HE WALKED BACK TOWARDS HIS VILLAGE.

WITH THIS I SHALL SWEEP AWAY THE SORROW OF DEATH FROM MY VILLAGE. THERE WILL NOT BE A SINGLE UNHAPPY HOUSE THERE.

MY IMPORTANCE WILL GROW IN THE VILLAGE. I MAY EVEN BE MADE THE HEADMAN!

SUDDENLY, HE BEGAN TO HAVE DOUBTS.

BUT SUPPOSING THE GODDESS WAS ONLY TEASING ME? SUPPOSING THESE ARE JUST ORDINARY LEAVES AND...

JUST THEN HE SAW A DEAD TIGER LYING IN HIS PATH.

AH! I CAN TEST THESE LEAVES ON THIS DEAD ANIMAL.

WITHOUT STOPPING TO THINK, THE FOOLISH, THOUGH LEARNED, BRAHMAN CRUSHED THE LEAVES IN HIS PALMS...

...AND SPRINKLED THE JUICE OVER THE TIGER.

THE TIGER STIRRED TO LIFE...

HM...M...M! I'M HUNGRY.

THE FEMALE PARROT AND THE HUNTER

THERE ONCE LIVED A FEMALE PARROT ON A BIG TREE IN A FOREST. IN THE HOLLOW OF ANOTHER TREE NEAR BY, LIVED A VENOMOUS SERPENT.

ONE DAY, THE FEMALE PARROT LAID SOME EGGS...

...AND SAT TENDERLY ON THEM. UNKNOWN TO HER, A HUNTER WAS CAREFULLY WATCHING HER FROM ANOTHER TREE.

AH! SHE HAS MOVED FROM THE NEST. A GOOD SIGN.

THEN ONE DAY THE HUNTER HEARD THE CHEEP OF FLEDGELINGS.

CHEEP CHEEP

THIS IS MY LUCKY DAY. THE EGGS HAVE HATCHED. THEY'LL FETCH A TIDY SUM.

CHEEP! CHEEP!

QUIET, LITTLE ONES. I'LL SOON BRING YOU SOME FOOD.

WHEN THE PARROT FLEW OFF, THE HUNTER CLIMBED THE TREE...

...AND PUT HIS HAND INTO THE NEST.

CHEEP! CHEEP!

JUST THEN, THE FEMALE PARROT RETURNED.

ALAS! HE'S OUT TO SNATCH MY YOUNG ONES.

WEEPING BITTERLY, SHE FLEW NEAR THE HUNTER'S FACE.

ARE THERE NO BIRDS ELSEWHERE? MY LITTLE ONES HAVE NOT OPENED THEIR EYES AS YET. WHY SHOULD ANYBODY WANT TO HARM THEM?

SHE LED HIM TO THE TREE WHERE THE SERPENT LIVED AND POINTED TO THE HOLLOW.

PUT YOUR HAND INTO THAT HOLLOW AND TAKE ALL THE GOLD YOU WANT.

THE HUNTER HARDLY WAITED FOR HER TO FINISH.

THE NEXT MOMENT—

EA...A...H! I'VE BEEN BITTEN BY A SERPENT.

WITHIN MINUTES THE POISON SPREAD ALL OVER HIS BODY AND HE FELL DEAD.

IT'S A PITY HE HAD TO DIE. BUT THAT WAS THE ONLY WAY I COULD SAVE MY YOUNG ONES.

THE END

THE FOOLISH CRANE

LONG AGO, THERE LIVED AN OLD CRANE NEAR A LAKE ON THE BANK OF WHICH WAS A TALL COCONUT TREE.

THE LAKE BEING ALMOST DRY, THERE WERE JUST ENOUGH FISH FOR THE CRANE TO LIVE ON. BUT THE OLD CRANE WAS VAIN ABOUT HIS TREE AND HIS LAKE.

HOW I WISH OTHER CRANES TOO WOULD COME AND SETTLE HERE AND SEE HOW LUCKY I AM.

THEN ONE DAY, HE SAW A FLOCK OF CRANES FLYING PAST HIS LAKE.

STOP! STOP. PLEASE STOP.

THE LEADER OF THE FLOCK SAW HIM.

THAT OLD BIRD IS CALLING OUT TO US. LET'S FLY DOWN AND SEE WHAT HE WANTS.

WHEN THEY REACHED THE BANK—

AH! I'M SO GLAD YOU HEARD ME. PLEASE BE MY GUESTS. YOU CAN PERCH ON THE COCONUT TREE AND EAT THE FISH IN THE LAKE.

HE IS GOOD BUT FOOLISH. HE WANTS TO IMPRESS US, BUT AT WHAT COST! HE WILL STARVE TO DEATH IF WE ACCEPT HIS INVITATION.

SO, ON BEHALF OF HIS FLOCK, THE WISE LEADER DECLINED THE OFFER.

WE ARE PLEASED BY YOUR AFFECTION FOR US. BUT PLEASE PERMIT US TO GO OUR WAY.

YES, OUR WISE LEADER IS RIGHT. WE ARE SO MANY OF US.

WHAT YOU HAVE IS SUFFICIENT ONLY FOR YOU. PLEASE PERMIT US TO GO ELSEWHERE.

IF YOU DON'T ACCEPT MY HOSPITALITY, I WILL GIVE UP MY LIFE.

THE WISE LEADER HAD NO CHOICE BUT TO ACCEPT.

ALL RIGHT. WE SHALL BE YOUR GUESTS.

COME, THEN. LET US GO TO MY TREE.

SO THE CRANES ALL WENT TO THE COCONUT TREE.

THE OLD CRANE FELT QUITE PROUD AND STRUTTED ABOUT IN HIS VANITY.

MAKE YOURSELVES COMFORTABLE AND WHEN YOU ARE HUNGRY PLEASE HELP YOURSELVES TO THE FISH IN MY LAKE. THERE IS ENOUGH FOR ALL OF YOU.

THE FLOCK OF CRANES TOOK HIM AT HIS WORD AND BEGAN FEASTING ON THE FISH.

I BET I CAN EAT MORE THAN YOU.

I BET YOU CAN'T.

I'VE EATEN SIX FISH ALREADY. CAN EITHER OF YOU BETTER THAT?

WITH ALL THEIR BETTING THEY SOON FINISHED ALL THE FISH IN THE LAKE.

OH, DEAR! NOT A SINGLE FISH LEFT. WHAT SHALL I GIVE THEM IN THE EVENING? WHAT SHALL I EAT WHEN THEY ARE GONE?